D1101062

I Was There...

SHAKESPEARE'S GLOBE

For John and Laraine Harris
with love

While this book is based on real characters and actual historical events, some situations and people are fictional, created by the author.

1053727/JF

WESTMEATH COUNTY LIBRARY

Scholastic Children's Books
Euston House,
24 Eversholt Street
London, NW1 1DB, UK

A division of Scholastic Ltd
London ~ New York ~ Toronto ~ Sydney ~ Auckland
Mexico City ~ New Delhi ~ Hong Kong

First published in the UK by Scholastic Ltd, 2014

Text copyright © Valerie Wilding, 2014

Illustrations by Peter Cottrill
© Scholastic Ltd, 2014

All rights reserved.

ISBN 978 1407 14506 8

Printed and bound by CPI Group (UK) Ltd, Croydon, CR0 4YY

1 3 5 7 9 10 8 6 4 2

The right of Valerie Wilding to be identified as the author of this work has been asserted by her in accordance with the Copyright, Designs and Patents Act, 1988.

This book is sold subject to the condition that it shall not, by way of trade or otherwise be lent, resold, hired out, or otherwise circulated without the publisher's prior consent in any form or binding other than that in which it is published and without a similar condition, including this condition, being imposed upon the subsequent purchaser.

I Was There...

SHAKESPEARE'S GLOBE

Valerie Wilding

SCHOLASTIC

CHAPTER ONE

I went home with my dog, Hoppy, one pot of honey, three duck eggs, a cut lip and a bashed nose.

Instead of sympathy, all I got from Aunt Meg was, 'Where is the fish, Billy? You didn't get the fish? Now what shall we do?'

'Big Tom was lurking by the fish stall, and I didn't want any more of this,' I said, catching blood drips in my hand.

Just then, Mother came through the back door and saw me. She dropped her laundry basket, grabbed a clean rag and dabbed at my face.

'Those ruffians again?' she asked.

I nodded. 'Big Tom. He tore my jerkin, too.'

'Never mind,' said Mother. 'Jerkins mend, so do lips and noses.'

I smiled. It made my mouth sting.

'He didn't get the fish!' wailed Aunt Meg. 'What will we have for dinner?'

'We'll have fish!' said Mother, crossly. She hates it when my aunt falls to pieces, as she calls it. Mother is strong-minded. She has to be, with Father away so much.

'Billy and I will go to the market together while Susan is having her nap,' she said. 'There will be plenty of fish left.'

Susan is my little sister. She's quite sweet, but everyone fusses around her because she's always getting sore throats or fevers.

'I'll put Hoppy in his doghouse,' I said. 'Another walk would be too much for his gammy leg.'

As Mother and I set off, I told her what happened.

'Big Tom and his mates were throwing stones at a kitten,' I said, 'so I picked it up and put it behind a wall. Then they started on me, so I punched Big Tom.'

'Good boy, Billy,' said Mother. She likes kittens. 'I'm glad you stand up to those ruffians.'

I stopped talking then, because my lip hurt.

I call Aunt Meg's cottage 'home' but it's not really our home. I hate it here. It's all grass and trees and cows, and there's nothing to do. I wish I was back in London. It's the finest and biggest city in the world. From our house in Little Thames Lane it's a long walk to the countryside. Thank goodness.

But we must stay here, because London is full of plague. The last outbreak was in 1593, when I was little. All I can remember are bells being rung during burials, and seeing carts taking bodies away.

When it broke out this time, Mother stopped me seeing my friends. No visitors came, and people wouldn't speak to others without covering their mouths and noses. Everyone is terrified they'll find huge buboes swelling under their arms, or hideous black spots. If they do, they're likely to die horribly. Hundreds of people have died already. There are red crosses on doors all over the city warning, 'Plague here – keep away'. That's why Mother decided that we should come to stay with her sister at Kinglake Manor.

Sounds grand, does it not? Me – William Watkins of Kinglake Manor.

Of course, we're not staying in the manor house! Aunt Meg and Uncle Jem live in Gate Cottage on the Kinglake estate. My uncle is the gamekeeper and my aunt does sewing for the ladies of the big house. She's pretty, and fun when she's not fretting about fish.

It's not my fault I'm unhappy here. Big Tom and his mates make my life miserable. They call me 'maggot head' or 'Willy goat brain'.

I know why. I cannot catch frogs with my bare hands or trap rabbits, and I've no wish to climb trees to steal apples.

Catch frogs? I'm sure I could, but who would want to? As for trapping rabbits, it's not worth it. Uncle Jem keeps us supplied with meat. And I'm definitely not going to steal fruit, or anything else. I'd never take the chance. Imagine being locked up and whipped or, worse – hanged! Zooks, even being put in the pillory for people to pitch rotten cabbages at you would be bad enough.

So they pick on me because I'm different. I don't want to be a farmhand or butcher, like them, or go to sea like my father. I want to be a player. I want to be a player, acting on the stage at the Globe playhouse in London!

I remember telling Uncle Jem about my ambition.

'That's stupid, lad,' he said.

'It's not,' I told him. 'I've even stood on the stage.'

'Ha! You're jesting!' he said.

'It's true,' I said. 'I help at the Globe.'

'Doing what, lad?'

'Anything. They call me Billy-Odd-Job,' I said proudly. 'And Master Burbage and Master Shakespeare said that one day I can have a part.'

He didn't believe me. But they did say so. And I believe them. One day, I'll have a part in a play by Master William Shakespeare!

As Mother and I crossed the bridge into town, I said, 'I wish we were back in London.'

'So do I,' she said, 'in our own lovely house, with Jane helping to look after us, but we can't be.'

Jane was our maid and not more than a year older than me, so she was fun. She left London, too, to live with her family in Kingston, a village further up the River Thames.

Mother smiled. 'At least you have Hoppy.'

That's true. I'd never have had him if I'd stayed in London.

We crossed Limping Lane, which made me smile, because that's what Hoppy does. Limps! Actually, he runs with a funny little hop, because of his gammy leg. He was attacked by a big dog when he was a pup. The stable man at the manor gave him to me.

Hoppy's the cleverest little dog in the world. I've taught him to beg, shut the door, and dance on his hind legs. If I clap twice, he bares his teeth and growls, looking so fierce. Yet the only thing he would ever bite is a bone!

I looked at the tiny cottages and tiny lanes in the tiny town. How much longer would we have to stay with Aunt Meg? I was bored in the country. I missed helping at the Globe. How would I ever become a player if I never went near the playhouse? The plague was ruining my life.

CHAPTER TWO

Mother pointed along Cake Lane, which opened into the market place. 'A crowd's gathering,' she said, as more people headed that way talking excitedly.

I walked faster, but Mother stopped me. 'Come in here,' she said, pulling me into the apothecary's shop.

'Good day, Mistress,' said Master Bottell. 'May I make something for you?'

The apothecary was polite to Mother, because she looks like quality. That's what Aunt Meg said, in a very sharp voice. She is jealous of Mother's clothes. Father is secretary to a rich merchant, and they go to far-away countries to buy silk. Mother gets so much gorgeous stuff to make gowns that she often gives some to Aunt Meg, who shouldn't grumble.

'Nothing, I thank you,' said Mother. 'Such a crowd...'

'I understand.' He fetched her a stool. 'But they are simply excited because an acting company is in town.'

'Acting company?' I said. 'Do you mean a company of players, sir?'

'I do.'

My heart leapt! Plays, in this very town, just like at the Globe! Well, not as grand as at the Globe, but plays all the same.

'Which company, sir?' I asked.

'The King's Men, no less. They will be several days here. Have you watched a play, boy?'

'Yes, sir!' I said. 'My father permits me to help at the Globe playhouse in London. It belongs to the Chamberlain's Men. Father says it's better that I work for Master Shakespeare and Master Burbage than run around the streets making mischief. He went to school with William Shakespeare in Stratford upon the Avon and—'

'That's enough, William,' said Mother.

When she calls me William, I know she means it. I didn't want a cuff round the ear to go with my cut lip and bashed nose. She dislikes me being at the Globe, but cannot disobey Father's wishes. It annoys her when I speak of it.

But the apothecary said, 'You know William Shakespeare?'

'I do, sir.'

'William Shakespeare, the poet? The great play writer?'

'Yes, sir,' I said.

'That's *enough*,' said Mother. 'Master Bottell doesn't want to hear any more about William Shakespeare.'

He seemed most interested to me.

'Mother, may I go and watch them preparing for the plays?' I begged.

'Certainly not.' She rose and turned, swishing her skirts. 'Come, we have fish to buy.'

By the time we'd bought our trout the crowd had thinned. Two of the company's carts were still waiting to enter the inn yard.

'I know what's in those baskets on the

first cart,' I told Mother. 'Gorgeous costumes.'

'Really?' she said, in a not-interested voice. 'I should have thought players too poor to have finery.'

'Wealthy people give clothes they do not want to their favourite players. Lords do that. Ladies, too.'

Mother raised her eyebrows. 'Lords and ladies go to watch the plays?'

'They do,' I said. 'Nobles love plays. Lord Hunsdon, the Lord Chamberlain, is the company's patron. And Queen Elizabeth herself used to invite the Chamberlain's Men to perform in her palaces,' I said. 'She loved Master Shakespeare's plays above all.'

It was true about the palaces, but I do not know if Will Shakespeare's plays were her favourites. No matter. Mother cannot know otherwise.

She considered my words, then said,

'Queen Elizabeth is dead. Come, let's go before the fish rots and gives your aunt something else to complain about.'

I swung the basket as I walked. I felt so excited. It was months since I'd been in the playhouse. Now we could watch a play right here in town! And not just one, because players put on different plays each day. I remember the Chamberlain's Men acting *Julius Caesar* one afternoon after rehearsing *A Midsummer Night's Dream* that morning, and they would act another the next day! A player might perform a murder in ancient Rome after spending the morning as the king of the fairies or a poor weaver with the head of an ass, called Bottom!

I remember men and boys sitting in out-of-the-way places in the Globe, clutching pieces of paper. The words they would speak were written on those papers. They would stare at the sky with their lips moving as they struggled to learn them by heart.

I am good at learning by heart, so it will be no problem for me when I am a player.

For that is what I will be. And nothing will stop me.

1053727/JF

CHAPTER THREE

It was only as I shut Aunt Meg's hens in for the night that I remembered Master Bottell calling the company of players the King's Men. Now Queen Elizabeth is dead, we have a king called James. He is probably the patron of the King's Men. A king is higher than a chamberlain, so they must be very good.

I had to see them perform. I had to!

I raced inside, nearly tripping over Hoppy, who was curled up beside Aunt Meg. She looked fed up, because Uncle Jem was snoring by the fire, and Mother was mending my jerkin.

'For goodness sake, stop tearing around,' said Mother. 'Do some drawing.'

Aunt Meg sat up. 'Draw me, Billy!'

Not again, I thought. I went up to the

attic room where I sleep, and fetched the leather bag Father gave me when he last came home. Inside was a wooden box of charcoal that he bought on his journey, and a thick pile of paper from the ship. The paper has sketches and writing on one side, but the other side is perfect for drawing. Charcoal is messy, but good for sketching, and I love to draw.

Father said when I'm older I can go to sea with an explorer, and draw the things we discover, to show learned men back in England.

No. I will be a player, and bring pleasure to everyone who sees me. Players bring words alive. I have seen Master Shakespeare's words written down, and they do not have half the life they have when he speaks them.

I brought my drawing things to the fire, and fetched Mother a cup of ale. I wanted to please her.

First I drew an eye then, next to it, a heart. Finally, I drew a sheep. I wanted it to be a female sheep, but all sheep look the same, so I drew a riband round her neck, tied in a bow.

I took my drawing to Mother.

'What is this?' she asked.

'A letter,' I said. 'A letter to you.'

'But there is no writing,' she said.

Of course not. Mother cannot read, so what was the point of writing words?

'Read the pictures,' I said. 'What is this?'

'An eye.'

'And this?'

'A heart.'

'And what is a heart full of?' I asked.

'Love,' she said.

I pointed to the sheep. 'And this?'

She thought for a moment. 'A sheep, with a bow round its neck, so … it must be a ewe.'

'That is right!' I said. 'So, what does your letter say?'

She looked again. 'Eye … love … ewe… Oh, Billy, it says "I love you!"' She hugged me. 'You sweet boy!'

I waited a while as Aunt Meg dozed and Mother sewed. She finished the jerkin, and picked up a chemise.

'I wonder,' I said, quietly, so as not to wake my aunt.

'Wonder what?'

I took a deep breath. 'May we go to the play tomorrow?'

She sipped her ale. 'No.'

Without opening her eyes, Aunt Meg said sleepily, 'Why not?'

'Billy knows I disapprove of players. If it was not for him having his father's permission, he would not be allowed anywhere near the Globe.'

I wanted to cry. Why couldn't she understand?

I snapped my fingers. Hoppy got up obediently, and came to me. I gave him my signal to die for the king, and he lay down, perfectly still, while I drew him. The only sound was the *shch shch* of my charcoal, the crackle of the fire, and Aunt Meg's breathing.

I finished my drawing, and clicked with my tongue. Hoppy sprang up. I hugged him, feeling so miserable. One day, I thought. One day Mother will see me act, and she'll be proud of me.

But at that moment I didn't see how it could ever be possible. The thought brought tears to my eyes. I sniffed.

'Billy?' said Mother.

'Yes.'

'Look at me.'

'I don't want to.'

'Look at me!' she said.

I turned my face to her.

She gazed at me for a few moments, then said, 'All right.'

'What do you mean?'

'I'll take you to the play. You have little to entertain you here, I know. I also know how much it means to you. I suppose that if your father were here, he would take you.'

I leapt up, throwing my arms round her. 'Thank you!'

'But mind,' she said, 'no talking to players.'

I hardly slept that night. I felt so happy.

CHAPTER FOUR

I woke early next morning to find Mother still abed.

Aunt Meg said, 'Susan was sick during the night, but she's asleep now, so your mother is resting, too. Why not go and look for mushrooms, Billy? There might be some about.'

I ate some bread and drank two cups of milk. We have plenty of milk. Kinglake Manor has its own farm, and Uncle Jem and the farmer do swaps. We get milk, butter and cheese, and Uncle Jem gives him pheasants, rabbits and venison.

I took Aunt Meg's collecting basket, called Hoppy and set off. Gathering mushrooms was an excellent excuse for wandering around. I hate the countryside, but I like the animals. I have seen badgers, foxes and hedgehogs, which are covered in prickles. I never saw anything like that in London. It is the strangest creature ever. When it is frightened, it rolls into a ball!

On the far side of Kinglake Stream there was a field where mushrooms sometimes grew.

We rounded the lake, left Kinglake Manor grounds, and followed the path over a hill.

I heard a sudden shout, followed by a shrill scream. It came from the foot of the wooded slope.

I hurtled downhill so fast my feet nearly got left behind, and burst out of the trees to see Big Tom poking something on the ground with his fishing pole. It looked like a bundle of clothes.

As Tom poked again, the bundle moved, and a terrified little face peeped out. It was a child!

'Stop!' I yelled. 'You're hurting him!'

Tom laughed, and poked the child again.

I ran at him, and shoved him in the back. He staggered forward and hit a tree with his shoulder.

'Get away, you doddypoll!' Tom bawled, his face red and angry. He swung at me.

I jumped clear, fell backwards, and scrabbled around, feeling for a stone or a broken branch – anything to defend myself with. My hands found only dried leaves.

Tom loomed over me. He raised the pole

back over his head and swung it down towards my face. I grabbed the pole with both hands, and swung it to the side. He stumbled in the same direction but, as he caught his balance, he pulled hard.

The pole slipped through my hands, leaving splinters of wood.

I yelped in pain, making Hoppy bark.

Hoppy! Of course! I clapped my hands.

Instantly, my little dog bared his teeth, snarling and growling. He looked quite menacing.

'Walk!' I ordered, pointing, and he walked his funny hopping walk towards Big Tom, still growling.

'Call him off!' he said, backing away.

The great oaf was just a coward.

'Not until you go,' I said.

Hoppy drew nearer to him, head low, lip curled above bared teeth.

Tom retreated. Slowly at first, then faster.

When he was far enough away, I called, 'Come!' to Hoppy.

I turned to the child. 'You're safe now,' I said. 'He's gone.'

The bundle uncurled, and a skinny little girl with long dark hair flung her arms around me.

'Thank you, master,' she said. 'You and your dog saved me from that 'orrible boy!' She glanced at Hoppy. 'Will 'e bite me?'

I laughed. 'No, he's a good—'

There was a crashing sound behind me. I turned to see a huge man charging out of the trees, brandishing a big stick. My heart seemed to stop.

'Put my Rosa down,' he roared.

The little girl ran towards him. 'Stop!' she shrieked. 'Stop, Pa!'

He crouched and hugged her, but his eyes never left me.

'What did 'e do to you, Rosa, my sweeting?' he said.

'Nuffin',' she replied, 'but 'e saved me from this other boy who was hurting me. This boy's a good 'un, honest.'

The man stood and strode towards me.

My feet wouldn't move. I couldn't speak.

The man hefted the stick into his left hand, and reached out with his right. 'I will shake your hand, boy, if you please,' he said. 'I thank you for helping my daughter. I won't forget.'

We walked through the woods together, Rosa between us. The man's name was Gilbert, and they were travelling people, going north to be with family. He wore baggy breeches and an embroidered jerkin over a full-sleeved shirt. On his head was a piece of bright green cloth, knotted at the back.

Rosa's skirt was made of layers of blue

and yellow materials, and her bodice had brightly coloured ribbons fastened on it.

'Are you gypsies?' I asked.

'We are like gypsies,' he said, 'but we are English-born, so no one can accuse us of being Egyptian. But for your sake, boy, it's best not to be seen with us.'

I knew that gypsies who were not born in England could be hanged, so I stopped and said, 'I must go. I am supposed to be finding mushrooms.'

'Nay, boy,' he said. 'I shall reward you for helping Rosa. Look, just here.'

He went to a hollowed-out yew tree, reached inside and pulled out a rabbit. He must have trapped it.

'For your supper,' he said. 'Now you need not hunt for mushrooms.'

He put the rabbit in my basket. I did not tell him we can have rabbit any day of the week.

I said goodbye and wished them a safe journey.

'Tell no one we are here,' said Gilbert. 'We will be gone tomorrow.'

I promised. Before I left, Rosa squeezed my hand. 'You're unhappy,' she said.

'It's this place.' I waved my arm in the direction of Gate Cottage and the town. 'You've seen what people can be like. That boy who attacked you did this,' I said, pointing to my cut lip. 'I don't belong here.'

'Why don't you move on?' she asked.

'Move on?'

'Yes, go where you wants to go. That's what we do.'

'Really?' I said.

'Yes, Pa says, why stay where you'se unhappy, when you can go where you'se happy?'

She squeezed my hand again. 'I likes you,' she said. 'I will see you again.'

I laughed. 'I don't expect so!'

Gilbert grinned. 'If Rosa says she will, then she will. She has the sight,' he said, tapping the middle of his forehead.

They disappeared into the trees. It was as if they had never been there.

I took the rabbit home and said I had found it. 'It's fresh,' I insisted, when Aunt Meg turned her nose up.

'Take it to Goody Wyse this afternoon,' she said. 'She will welcome meat for her pot.'

Mother came downstairs, carrying soiled bed linen. 'Susan is still being sick,' she said. 'She has a fever, too.'

'Billy,' said Aunt Meg, 'take the rabbit to Goody Wyse now. Ask her to kindly come and see Susan. She will likely have a potion to help her.'

This seemed silly. 'Goody Wyse's cottage is on the way to town,' I said. 'I'll take it when Mother and I go to the play.'

Silence.

Mother dropped the bedding on the table. 'How can you think of a stupid play when your sister is abed, sick?' she demanded. 'We're not *going* to the play!'

She picked up the linen and went outside, muttering. I caught the words, 'selfish', 'thoughtless' and 'wretched play'.

I did feel sorry for Susan, truly. But I felt sorrier for myself. I looked out of the door and called, 'May I go on my own, Mother?'

She didn't have to speak. Her face clearly told me the answer. So I took the rotten rabbit to Goody Wyse, though how she would eat it with only one tooth, I do not know.

She had a sore foot and could not walk, so I stood in her stuffy cottage, nearly fainting from the fire's heat, while she asked about Susan. She seemed to take hours mixing a potion, and I was never so glad to get home. Except it wasn't my home.

CHAPTER FIVE

I was so miserable that Aunt Meg felt sorry for me, and asked Mother to let me go that afternoon.

I listened from downstairs.

'Meg, there'll be bad characters in the crowd,' said Mother.

'This isn't London,' said my aunt. 'Everyone knows everyone else around here. None of us would steal from each other, or hurt each other.'

'Oh? Then what do you call Big Tom's behaviour to Billy? Kindness?' Mother said sharply.

Aunt Meg gave up and came downstairs. 'I tried, Billy,' she said, throwing carrots in the pottage pot. 'I'm sorry. I can imagine how you feel. I would like to see a play, too.'

'Were you going to come?' I asked.

'No, I was going to look after Susan,' my aunt replied, 'but your mother will look after her now she's so poorly.'

If Aunt Meg wanted to go, and Mother was looking after Susan, then perhaps...

'You could take me!' I cried.

Aunt Meg hadn't thought of that. Her face lit up!

She passed me the remains of yesterday's ham. 'Strip the meat off and throw the bone in the pot,' she said, hurrying upstairs. I heard Mother shushing her. Susan must have fallen asleep. There was much whispering, and eventually Aunt Meg ran down.

'Get your cap,' she said. 'We're going to the play!'

★

The middle of the day found Aunt Meg, wearing her finest yellow-flowered shawl, walking alongside me into town.

We were early enough to get a good place in the inn yard. It was nothing like the Globe on performance days. There weren't many food sellers, just a pie man and a girl trying to sell wrinkled apples.

The yard was a fraction of the size of the Globe's, as was the stage, which was tiny in comparison. It was raised to the height of a man's shoulder, so everyone could see the players. There was a curtain at the back, which was on a frame, forming a closed-in area behind the stage. In there the players would be changing into their costumes, and sorting out the properties. Props are things that go on stage, like chairs, thrones, crowns, even small things like letters. At the Globe there's a whole building behind the stage, called the tiring house.

A trumpet player blew a flourish,

announcing the start of the play.

When he lowered his instrument, I had such a surprise! It was old John Merry! He worked for the Chamberlain's Men, and one of his tasks was trumpeting. What was he doing with the King's Men? I couldn't believe he'd been thrown out of the Chamberlain's men. He was clever and well loved.

I was even more confused when the curtains parted and on to the stage strode Master Richard Burbage!

How could this be? Why was one of the owners of the Chamberlain's Men here? Were they all here? Pretending to be King's Men?

Master Burbage bowed and held his arms wide. 'Welcome, one and all,' he said in his rich voice. 'We are right glad to see so many good people come to our play. My father, James Burbage, built the theatre – the second-oldest playhouse in England.

Our company is from the *newest* playhouse in England – the Globe, in London – and we used to be the Chamberlain's Men.'

I held my breath as he continued.

'Following the sad death of our Sovereign Lady Queen Elizabeth, King James has honoured our company by becoming our patron. You good people are about to watch the most important company of players in the land – the King's Men!'

When the cheers died down, Master Burbage said, 'Our company played for King James in his palace at Christmas time.' He framed his face with his hands and continued, 'These faces you gaze at have been looked upon by royalty.'

The crowd were impressed. I was impressed, but also cross that I had been away when they played for the king. If I had been in London, I might have gone with them. Again I cursed the plague for ruining my life.

The play was *The Taming of the Shrew*, which I have seen before, but I hardly watched. I knew the story anyway. Bianca is sweet and gentle, and her sister Katherine is bad tempered and rude. Katherine must marry first, but no one wants her, until Petruchio, who wants a rich wife, decides she will suit, and sets about taming her.

While Aunt Meg was laughing at the play, I pondered how to persuade her to let me greet the players. I decided to ask her straight out.

I needn't have worried. The thought of meeting players made Aunt Meg quite excited. As the crowd moved away, we went towards the stage. She patted her hair, and straightened her bodice. Then she pinched her cheeks. Mother does that to make them look pink, but Aunt Meg did it too hard. She looked as if someone had slapped her.

As I reached the back of the curtained booth, Master Burbage appeared. He stared.

'Well, if it isn't young Billy-Odd-Job! Hey, men!' he called. 'See what I have found!'

Aunt Meg pushed close to me, so I

introduced her. Master Burbage bowed over her hand. 'Greetings, fair lady,' he said.

She fluttered her eyelashes so much I thought they might fly away.

The men patted me on the back, and said they had a hard time without me helping them. I felt myself go red. I was so pleased.

When they'd all gone to clear away the costumes and properties, Master Burbage said, 'I must say farewell now, Billy. There is much to do.' He bowed to Aunt Meg, who was as pink as a beetroot stain. 'Madam.'

She bobbed a curtsy. 'Good day, sir.'

It was now or never. 'Master?' I said.

'Hmm?'

'You and Master Shakespeare promised that one day I could be on stage. Not saying any words,' I gabbled, 'just walking on and being in the crowd. Can I? Can I do that here?'

He didn't answer.

'It would be good to practise in a small town, would it not?' I pleaded.

Master Burbage looked stern. Then, slowly, a grin spread across his face. 'Why not?' he said.

My heart leapt.

'Billy, you shall play a bystander in the market,' he said. 'All you must do is examine things on stalls and pretend to talk to stallholders. If a fight breaks out, and it will, you must look surprised, then fearful, and back away. Can you do that?'

'I can, sir,' I cried, as Aunt Meg clapped her hands in delight. 'Is the play *Romeo and Juliet*?'

Master Burbage raised his eyebrows. 'You are sharp, Billy-Odd-Job. It is, indeed. Now go. Be back in two days, an hour before we open, to don your costume.'

My heart swelled big enough to burst. I didn't think it was possible ever to be so happy.

'Billy!' he called after us. 'Your mother

must permit this. Your father, when he arranged for you to come to the Globe, said she does not love the playhouse.'

After a brief pause, I said, 'Yes, sir.'

As Aunt Meg and I walked away, she said, 'That could be a problem.'

I felt as if the sun had gone behind a dark grey cloud.

CHAPTER SIX

'No! No! No!'

'But Mother—'

'No buts, Billy! What would people think of you, on the stage like a common player?' she said, hacking onions into fat slices.

Aunt Meg murmured, 'I would be proud if my nephew was in a play.'

Mother stared at her. 'Are you mad? You know how players are thought of. Vagabonds, rascals—'

'Not these players,' said Aunt Meg. 'William Shakespeare is the greatest poet in the land, people say. And Master Burbage is a true gentleman, as well as a great player.'

Mother banged her knife down, making the onions bounce. 'Enough, Meg! I am sick of hearing about William Shakespeare. As for

Master Burbage, tell me, pray, how would *you* know he's a gentleman? Have you met him? No!'

'Yes,' said Aunt Meg.

She told Mother about our conversation with Master Burbage. Maybe *I* should have done that instead of bursting into the house, crying, 'They want me to act on the stage. Please say yes!'

Aunt Meg tried hard to change Mother's mind. 'Think how impressed people will be that my sister's boy is thought highly of by William Shakespeare and... and...'

'Richard Burbage,' I said.

'...Richard Burbage,' she finished, adding, 'They are important people in London. The King likes them, after all.'

Mother sat down, looking bemused. 'Will Shakespeare and the King...' she muttered to herself. 'Who would have thought it?'

‘Please?’ I begged.

‘Billy, don’t keep on,’ she said. ‘You know I don’t—’

Just then, Susan gave a long, wailing cry. That was the end of the conversation. I grabbed Mother’s oniony hand. ‘*Please*?’

She pulled away, wiped her hands and hurried upstairs. Just before she disappeared from view, she glanced back.

‘You may do it. But this once only. Never ask me again.’

I hugged Aunt Meg. ‘Thank you!’ I cried. ‘What heaven! Me! A player!’

Mother called for a damp cloth. ‘Susan’s fever is high,’ she said.

I fetched the cloth. As I gave it to her, I said, ‘May I go and tell Master Burbage I have your permission?’

‘Yes,’ she said, ‘but be back before dark and take care. I don’t suppose oh-so-wonderful

Master Burbage wants a player with a fat lip and bloody nose.'

I set off with Hoppy, thinking how this would wipe the smile off the faces of those ruffians who think I'm so useless.

As I walked, I had the feeling Hoppy and I weren't alone. Someone was behind me. Big Tom? I refused to turn round, because he'd say something like, 'Scared of your shadow, city boy?'

But then I felt a tug at my breeches. It was Rosa, the little gypsy girl. No, not 'gypsy'. If anyone heard that, she'd be in trouble.

'Good day to yer, Billy,' she said.

'Good day, Rosa!' I said.

'I didn't know if I should speak to yer,' she said.

'Of course you should,' I said. 'We're friends, are we not?'

She grinned. 'I likes you, Billy.'

Hoppy put his nose in her hand, and she tickled his ears.

'Rosa, why are you still here?' I asked. 'Your father said you would be gone.'

Her smile vanished. 'Me muvver is sick,' she said. 'She 'as to be well afore we can travel.'

'I'm sorry,' I said. 'I hope she is well soon.'

Rosa stopped. 'I'm going now. I just want to thank you for 'elping me. I will repay you.'

She slipped into the trees and was gone.

Once in town, I went straight to the inn yard, but there was no one around. I found the ostler in the stables.

'Pardon me,' I said. 'Where are the players?'

He picked up a brush. 'They be restin'. Keep that dog away from the 'orses.'

I signalled 'outside' and off Hoppy went.

'Would you give Master Burbage a message?' I asked.

He swept the brush along a horse's back. 'My job,' he said, 'is seein' to the 'orses, not carryin' messages.'

Thanks mightily, I thought, and went into the yard. A maid was sloshing water across the cobbles.

'Pardon me!' I called.

She looked up and grinned. 'What can I do for you?'

'Will you give a message to the players?'

Her eyes gleamed. 'That I will!'

'Tell Master Burbage that Billy-Odd-Job will be here on time, to act his part in the play.'

Her eyes widened. 'Are you a player, sir?'

I felt six-feet tall. 'That I am!' I said.

She bobbed a curtsy. 'I'll deliver your message now.'

As I turned out of the yard entrance, I was nearly run into by a man on horseback.

'Careful, boy!' said the rider, as his horse

danced to one side. 'You'll have me off, frightening my mount like that!'

'Sorry, sir,' I said.

He dismounted, pulled off his hat and banged it against the wall. Dust flew everywhere. When he turned I saw his face for the first time.

'Master Shakespeare!' I cried.

'Bless my soul! Billy-Odd-Job!' he said. 'What are you doing here?'

'We are living with relatives because of the plague and I don't like it in the country and I saw the play and Master—'

He held up a hand. 'Whoa! Slow down!'

I began again, explaining that Master Burbage had said I could be in *Romeo and Juliet*.

He smiled. 'I am returning from visiting my family in Stratford, and I am as excited as you to be back with the company. You still wish to be a player, Billy?'

'Oh sir, more than anything in the world,' I said.

He looked thoughtful. 'I remember when I was young,' he said. 'Your father and I made a pact – a promise to ourselves – that we would always follow our hearts. My heart told me I must be a player, and write plays.' He laughed. 'Your father wanted to see the world, and I wanted the world to see me!'

He gathered his horse's reins and led it towards the stables. I signalled to Hoppy to stay at my heel.

'I want to be a player so much, sir,' I said. 'My father understands. That's why he lets me help at the Globe. But Mother doesn't want me there.'

He handed the reins to the grumpy ostler. 'All things change, Billy,' he said. 'There's a time for everything.' He put his dusty hat on and clapped me on the shoulder. 'Now for a jug of ale!'

As he went to the inn door, I called. 'Two days, Master Shakespeare! I will be back in two days to play my part in *Romeo and Juliet*!'

He waved. 'I look forward to your performance, Billy-Odd-Job! And mark what I say – follow your heart and you will be on the stage of the Globe itself one day!'

I felt dizzy with delight. To act at the Globe had always been my dream. If William Shakespeare himself believed it would happen…!

CHAPTER SEVEN

The next morning was cold, with an icy wind. I sat in bed, huddled in my blanket, with Hoppy snuggled next to me. I thought of Rosa, and what it must be like to be travelling people in such weather. Then I remembered her sick mother.

I wished I could help them. What would they want?

That was easy. They'd want to get on with their journey. What was stopping them? Rosa's mother being ill.

I jumped up and struggled into my clothes.

Sick people need good food and warmth, Mother always says. I decided to take Rosa's mother some milk. I bet they never had milk. And cheese. I guessed they lived on berries and scraggy wild rabbits.

I fetched a jug of milk and wrapped a hunk of hard cheese in an old cloth, then set off for the woods with Hoppy.

I had no idea where they were camped, so we went to the place where I'd last seen Gilbert. I called his name softly.

Nothing.

'Rosa?' I called.

No answer.

I dared not call any louder for fear someone might hear and tell on them.

Then I remembered the hollow in the yew tree where Gilbert kept the rabbit. I found it with no trouble and put the jug and cheese in there. Then Hoppy and I went home.

When I got there, Goody Wyse was sitting by the fire talking to Mother, who was nursing Susan. The old lady's sore foot was wrapped in bandages and a strip of leather.

She reckons she can cure everyone else, I thought, so why can't she do something about her foot?

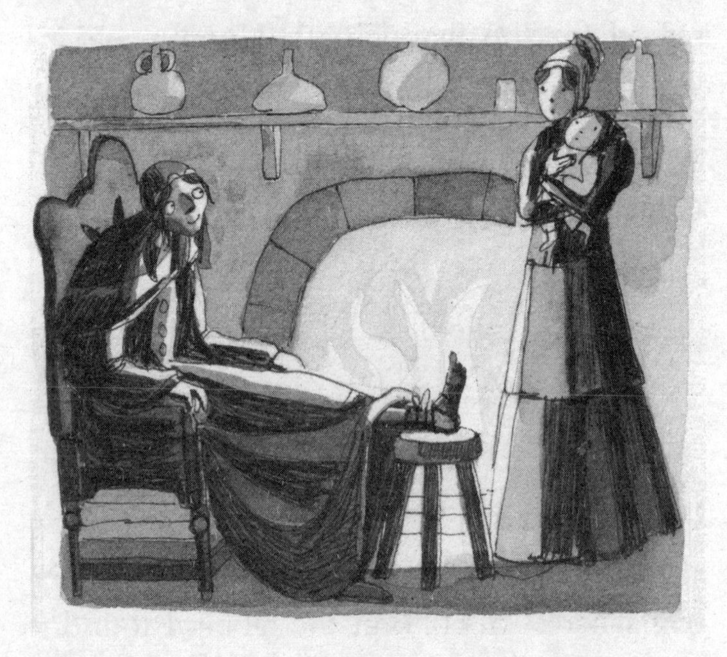

Aunt Meg had her back to me, rolling out pastry, listening to whatever Goody Wyse was blathering about.

The moment Mother saw me, she turned to Goody Wyse and put a finger to her lips.

Women's talk, I thought, and made for

the stairs. Goody Wyse didn't stop to draw breath and, out of her ramblings, the word 'players' jumped at me.

I stopped. 'What's that about players?'

Mother put Susan into Aunt Meg's floury arms and came to hug me.

'What? I said, pulling away.

'I'm sorry, Billy, my love,' she said.

For a heart-stopping moment I thought something had happened to Father, but Mother was not weeping, so the moment passed.

'Billy, I'm sorry,' she said again. 'Goody Wyse told us that the players... They're going back to London.'

I couldn't understand. 'Going? Why? They can't. The playhouses are closed.' I felt sick.

One day. My big chance was one day away, yet I was to be robbed of it.

Tears sprang to my eyes.

'The playhouses are opening again,'

Mother told me. 'The company is packing up already. The word from London is that the plague is officially over.'

Oh, those magical words! '*The plague is officially over.*'

I must have grinned, because Mother shook my shoulder. 'Billy? Are you all right?'

'Better than all right, Mother,' I cried. 'Don't you see? If the plague is over, we can go back to London, too! I'll be in the play there. At the Globe!'

I turned to run upstairs and start packing, but Mother caught my arm.

'Listen to me!' she said. 'Your sister is too ill to travel. You must be patient.' She put her face in her hands for a moment, then looked up. 'Believe me, I want nothing more than to be in our own home, but it's not possible. You have to understand. We're not going anywhere. Not for a while.'

CHAPTER EIGHT

I couldn't believe it. One minute my life was almost perfect and the next, everything was wrong.

I needed to see Master Burbage and Master Shakespeare. Maybe they weren't leaving until after tomorrow, after I'd played my part. Either way, I could tell them I'd be back in London as soon as Susan was better. I wanted their promise that I could still be in a play, on the stage, in front of an audience.

While Aunt Meg took her sewing up to the manor house, and Mother was singing to Susan, I crept out. I left Hoppy behind, because I had to run. I daren't be on the road after nightfall.

I had a shock when I reached the inn yard

and found the company already loading the carts. I asked old John Merry where Master Shakespeare was.

'Gone, lad,' he said. 'Will and some other players rode ahead to get the Globe ready, and Richard is leaving once everything's loaded. We last few will drive the wagon and carts to London tomorrow at first light.'

I tried to interrupt, but you can't stop old John once he starts.

'There's handbills to print and send out so people will know we're back, and the costumes that have been boxed up for months, they need airing. The food sellers must be told and—'

I gripped his arm. 'What about me?'

'You, lad? What about you?'

Just then Richard Burbage came out, carrying an armful of swords. He dumped them on the end cart as I caught up with him.

'Master Burbage!'

He turned. 'Billy-Odd-Job again!' he said. 'We could do with your help.'

I walked back to the inn door with him. 'Can't you stay,' I pleaded, 'just for another day or so?'

He hoisted up a leather bag containing crowns. 'The faster we get to London, the better,' he said, handing me the bag. Leaning forward, he said quietly, 'We've been away for so long because of the blasted plague that there's barely enough money to pay everyone. We get audiences of only a hundred or so in places like this,' he explained. 'There's much more money to be had in London. We can play to nigh on a couple of thousand people in one afternoon at the Globe.'

I put the leather bag on the cart, tucking it beneath a golden throne. 'Master Burbage,' I said, desperately. 'What about me playing that part in *Romeo and Juliet*?'

'Sorry, Billy. It won't be tomorrow. But it will be one day.' He laughed. 'Maybe at the Globe!'

Maybe. If I ever got there. If they did *Romeo and Juliet* again.

I hurried back to Gate Cottage, hoping to find my sister sitting up, eating pottage, and fit to travel.

I burst in. 'How is Susan?'

Instead of answering, Mother flew at me. 'Where have you been? I have worried until I was almost sick!'

I told her I went to say goodbye to the company.

'Do you not think I have enough to worry about, without you adding to it?' she demanded.

'How is my sister?' I asked.

Mother calmed down. 'Improving,' she said, then quickly added, 'but she is not fit to travel, so don't ask.'

I tried something different. 'Perhaps, until Susan is better, you could take me back to London, then return for her. Aunt Meg would look after her and—'

Mother's jaw dropped, and I caught sight of my aunt and uncle's shocked faces.

I looked from one to the other. 'It wouldn't be for long. You could be back in a few days.'

'How can you be so selfish?' Mother demanded. 'How would you like to be left behind when you were ill?'

I didn't need to answer. Mother was still ranting.

'You think only of yourself!' she said, and turned her back. Then she began to mutter.

'...London ... few days indeed ... all about himself ... poor Susan...'

She buried her face in her apron. I felt bad then, so I tugged at her arm.

'I'm sorry,' I said. 'Truly. I do care about Susan. It's just that I did so want to be in the play.' My eyes watered. I blinked hard, but Mother had noticed.

Her face softened. 'I know, Billy,' she said. 'And if you and your father have your way, I'm sure you will one day. But not yet.'

We ate then, and afterwards, as I cleared

the table, Aunt Meg said, 'Billy, did you put an empty jug outside the door?'

'No.'

'I can't understand how it got there,' said Aunt Meg. She put the bread away. 'Funny thing,' she added, 'there was a rose hip in it. Just one.'

In spite of feeling so upset, I smiled. Rosa … rose … rose hip. Rosa and Gilbert had found the milk and cheese. I hoped it had helped.

I thought about Rosa again when I was in bed. I remembered something she'd said.

'Go where you wants to go. Why stay where you'se unhappy, when you can go where you'se happy?'

I sat bolt upright.

Did I dare?

CHAPTER NINE

As the first glimmer of dawn appeared, I stole downstairs with a picture letter I'd done for Mother.

There was an eye, then a picture of me on a cart beside a milestone saying 'London 10 miles'. I did not actually know the distance, but that would do. Then I'd drawn a globe, and finally, a picture of me on a stage. I hoped it would say to her, 'I have gone to London with the company, to the Globe, so I can be on stage.'

I ended with my pictures for 'I love you'. Then I burned all the old drawings I'd left lying around, and put my letter on the table.

I took half a loaf, which was a bit stale, and some wrinkled apples from the apple store.

It hurt to leave Hoppy behind, but I

needed to reach town before the company left, and he couldn't run that fast.

I almost flew down the road but, even so, I was too late.

The yard was empty. The company had left.

As I walked slowly back into the market place, a voice said, 'You looking for the players?'

It was the grumpy ostler.

'I was,' I said. 'But they've gone.'

He gestured with his thumb. 'They can only be a mile up the London road. Young lad like you could catch up with 'em in no time.'

My grin must have nearly split my face in half! 'Thank you!' I cried, and I raced towards the London road.

I didn't stop running until I saw the wagon and carts lumbering along ahead of me. I slipped into the trees at the roadside to think what to do. If I asked them to take me, they might refuse. That would be that. But if I stowed away, they would take me without knowing.

The last cart was full of props. Even though it was covered by sacking, I could tell what it was by all the lumps and bumps sticking out. Old John Merry was driving it, and the way he slumped in his seat suggested he was half asleep.

I was wondering how to sneak on to the cart when I felt a familiar tug at my breeches. I nearly jumped out of my skin!

'Rosa!' I whispered. 'What are you doing here?'

'Nuffin',' she said. 'Just walkin' about. You're going then? Going where you'se happy?'

I'd just finished explaining my plan, when Gilbert slipped through the trees, clutching a handful of duck eggs.

'What you up to?' he asked.

Rosa quickly told him. 'He 'ad to leave 'is dog behind,' she added, ''cos of his lame leg. Now 'e has to get on the cart. I thought I'd try the crying trick. What d'you think, Pa?'

'Reckon that would do it,' he said. 'You carry on, Rosa, my pet. I'll see you later. I got something to do.'

I watched him melt into the trees. When I turned back, Rosa was gone!

The train of carts was rounding a bend. I slipped through the trees, keeping pace with the rear cart, when suddenly, the driver of the big front wagon gave a shout.

'Woah!' he cried. 'Hold fast!'

The carts stopped, and then I heard it. Rosa's voice, crying, wailing.

I moved to the side so I could see what she was up to. She was sitting in the middle of the road in front of the lead wagon, howling her eyes out.

'I lost me penny!' she bawled. 'Aow, aow, I lost me penny.'

Old John shouted from the back, 'What's amiss?'

'Little girl lost her penny!' came the reply. 'She won't move!'

Old John Merry swore, then called, 'Give her a penny quick, and let's be on our way.'

While they fussed over Rosa and her penny, I darted to the back of the props cart, and slid beneath the musty-smelling sacking.

My heart thumped, and there was pounding in my ears.

After a few moments, the cart jerked into motion.

We'd only travelled a few yards when a corner of the sacking was lifted, revealing Rosa's mischievous little face. She walked behind the cart, crouched down so old John wouldn't see her if he turned round, which was unlikely. He was probably dozing off again.

'Thank you, Rosa,' I whispered. 'One day I will write a play, and I will name the heroine Rosa. She'll be brave and clever, like you.'

She grinned. 'Travel safely,' she said. 'I will see you again, one day.'

The sacking dropped.

We moved so slowly I knew it would be a long journey. I tried to get comfortable, but a sword stuck into my back. I pushed it aside and felt for the leather bag I'd stuffed beneath the throne. I found it and pulled out the crowns. Rolled up, the bag made a pillow for my head.

I wished they'd hurry. After what seemed ages, we'd probably covered a mile at most.

I heard soft footsteps at the back of the cart. Then a chink of light revealed a big gnarled hand, shoving a cloth-wrapped package beneath the sacking.

I froze. What was happening?

My heart thumped. In a moment I would be discovered. We were still so close to Kinglake Manor that I'd be bound to be sent home, in disgrace.

The sacking lifted a little higher, and my heart thumped harder, because the next thing that was thrust towards me was my little dog. Hoppy! Gilbert's grinning face appeared. He, like Rosa, was crouching

behind the cart, walking to keep up with it.

'Thought you'd be better off with company, lad,' he whispered. 'Weren't no trouble getting him. I'm good with dogs, me.'

'Thank you, Gilbert,' I whispered, as my face was licked all over.

And he was gone.

I settled down, hugging Hoppy.

We were on our way to London, together.

CHAPTER TEN

The horrible, bumpy journey took much longer than I expected. I didn't bargain for the drivers stopping overnight at an inn. They took turns guarding the carts, and it was only when old John Merry was on guard that Hoppy and I had a chance to get out for a pee, and to stretch our legs.

I was grateful for Gilbert's little package. Inside were three chicken legs, which I ate, trusting they weren't from any of Aunt Meg's hens. I gave Hoppy the remaining chunks of meat, which I could not identify.

Next morning, we set off early and, before long, I heard the sound of more carts trundling along, and the pounding of horses' hooves. The road was growing busier, and I guessed we were nearing the city. I knew when we passed through the gate in London's wall, because the rattling of the cart echoed for a moment. The worst bit of the journey began then, as the cart clattered badly over cobbles, and everything shifted about. I got clouted on the head by a shield, and I felt sick from being thrown about so much.

And the voices! Street sellers shouting their wares, people arguing and swearing, children crying or laughing. I had forgotten how crowded London was. In the country you could walk a mile and only see sheep or cows.

I had also forgotten the stinks of the city. In the country everything smelled cleaner and fresher. Not so here. I knew the road would be slimy from animal poo and rotten vegetables and all manner of rubbish.

I dared not look out in case a passer-by shouted to old John that someone was hiding in his cart, but I knew when we reached the river. I could smell it. I had never thought of it as a bad smell before. Would I get used to it again? I wondered.

The noises changed, too, down by the river. Instead of street sellers' cries, I heard sailors and wharfmen, shouting things like, 'Heave!' and 'Hold fast!'

And then there were cheers. I wondered why, but quickly realized that people were cheering because the company had returned.

Suddenly, the cart ran on smooth ground, then I felt it move in a circle. We were in the Globe! I could not see it, but I remembered it clearly. A round, black and white building, with big double doors, close to the river's south bank.

Voices called greetings, and someone offered the drivers a jug of ale. What wouldn't I have given for a drink?

It felt late in the day to me, so I didn't

know if the carts would be unloaded or left till morning. I prayed they'd be left, so I could sneak away. Then, when I appeared before Masters Shakespeare and Burbage, they would think my mother and sister had returned to London, too.

I was lucky.

'See to the horses, men, and get the costumes inside,' said a voice. 'Leave the rest until the morrow. Go home and sleep.'

I hugged Hoppy. 'We'll get out soon,' I whispered, 'once all is quiet.'

When the voices had stopped, I listened for the big double doors to shut. I counted to a hundred and then one more hundred, before lifting the sacking.

The playhouse was silent. The stage, bare of actors and props, jutted out into the great yard, and the covered benches ranged around the walls were empty. All the cushions had been stored away. The light was fading and the first stars twinkled above me. It would soon be dark and I had nowhere to go. Our house was locked, with the windows boarded up, to stop thieves getting in. I dared not go to the neighbours in case they'd had plague in their houses.

I tried the big playhouse door that opened on to the outside. It was locked. So was the door to the tiring house – that's where the players dress in their attire for the plays, and where props are kept. The arches from the stage into the tiring house were boarded up. That was a shame. I could have slept comfortably in there.

I was just deciding which of the audience's benches I would sleep on, when I remembered something. Something secret.

A trapdoor in the stage floor that could drop down, leaving a hole through which a ghost or devil might appear. The audience couldn't see it. I knew that if you went down through the hole, you could get into the tiring house! During the day it's busy, with players dashing in and out, and wigs being flung around, musicians running up and down stairs to the balcony, and sometimes, if Master

Shakespeare makes last-minute changes to his play, the scribe is frantically writing out words for the players to learn quickly.

I climbed on to the stage and knelt by the trapdoor. What a fool I was! The bolt was underneath.

I needed to insert something thin between the boards, and try to slide the bolt across. It was kept well greased so it worked noiselessly.

I glanced at Hoppy, sitting silently opposite me. He was staring over my shoulder. The skin on my back prickled as I realized someone was behind me. I froze in fear, unable to move, as I imagined a dagger being plunged into my back.

I stared at my dog, my only hope of help. 'Ho-Hoppy...' I stammered.

A hand grabbed my shoulder.

I was sure I was going to die, when a voice from behind said, 'What in the name of—'

The hand spun me round. 'Billy-Odd-Job!'

I looked into the face of William Shakespeare.

★

I told the truth.

'So do I have this aright, Billy?' said Master Shakespeare. 'You ran away from your aunt's home? Your mother does not know you are here?'

'She does, sir,' I said quickly. 'I left a letter, saying where I was going.'

He relaxed a little. 'In that case, you may sleep here. There is a mattress I sometimes use. You can curl up behind the scribe's table. It is the warmest part of the tiring house – the least draughty, at any rate.'

I knew that. The scribe had to be warm or he could not write clearly.

'Can Hoppy stay, too, sir?' I asked.

Master Shakespeare smiled. 'Of course. You must not be entirely alone. The outer doors will be locked, so you will be quite safe.' He picked up his keys. 'You must be hungry,' he said. 'I will buy some food for you.'

He stopped at the tiring house door. 'Richard Burbage gave you a part in *Romeo and Juliet*?'

I nodded.

'We are doing that play shortly,' he said.

A thrill ran through me. Everything had been worthwhile! I couldn't stop grinning.

'But,' Master Shakespeare continued, 'when Burbage learns what you have done, he will almost certainly change his mind.'

CHAPTER ELEVEN

I spent a miserable night listening to rats scurrying beneath the floorboards, and dreading what morning would bring. Surely they wouldn't send me away?

Would they?

As the tiring men arrived and began their various tasks, I made myself useful. I thought it best to have people thinking well of me.

The players came in, cursing the damp weather, until finally Master Burbage arrived with Master Shakespeare, deep in conversation. Eventually Richard Burbage glanced at me, then spoke to Master Shakespeare, who nodded, and came over.

I made tears come into my eyes, like I've seen older boys do when they play women's parts.

'Richard is angry, Billy,' said Master Shakespeare. 'I have written to your mother – the inn people will know where she lives, no doubt. I have assured her that we did not make you leave home and come to the Globe. I cannot risk her accusing us of kidnap—'

'I am sure she would not, sir,' I said. 'There was the letter I left for her.'

He nodded. 'I had forgotten that. Even so, you have done wrong. However, you may stay here, as you have nowhere else to go, but you must work.'

'I will, sir, I will!'

'The work will be hard,' said Master Shakespeare. 'And it will be long. Oh, one other thing, Billy.'

'Yes, sir?'

'Those tears in your eyes,' he said. 'Real or faked?'

I hung my head, ashamed that he had

caught me out.

'Faked, sir,' I said. 'I am truly sorry.'

He put his hand under my chin and tilted my face up. He was smiling!

'I believed they were real,' he said. 'That was fine acting.'

I treasured those words over the next two long, hard days. I spent the mornings sweeping, scrubbing and cleaning everything that stood still. All the time I kept an ear and an eye on the players as they rehearsed. I listened, watched and learned.

Each afternoon, a flag of red, black or white was hoisted to announce whether the play would be a history, tragedy or comedy. Just before it was due to start the trumpeter played a blast to warn latecomers to hurry to pay the gatherer a penny, which he would put through the slot in his money box. Those who could afford it paid an extra penny and took their seats. As the crowd poured in, the noise grew, and the yard filled with groundlings, who had to stand, and food sellers, all chatting, laughing or calling to each other. Some leaned forward to gaze at the heavens. That's what we call the ceiling above the stage. It is painted with a sun and moon and stars, and is supported by two marble pillars. Well, they *look* like marble, but they are really made of wood, cleverly painted.

It was so exciting!

Soon I was busy showing nobles to the lords' rooms high on either side of the stage, and I fetched cushions for those on the benches who were willing to pay an extra penny not to get a stiff behind.

During the performance, I stood at the back of the lords' rooms, ready to fetch food or drinks for anyone who wanted them.

After the play, when the audience had left, I would take a stiff brush and a bucket of water outside, and scrub down where men had gone outside to pee in corners. That was really the job of Nick Ratter, who is well named. He has a face like a rat, and he does the dirtiest jobs in exchange for free ale. The trouble is, he drinks his ale too quickly, then he turns against me, and orders me to do his work. I do not complain, ever. I want the company to think well of me.

They do not take kindly to grumblers. A company must work together for the good of the play, Master Burbage says.

After the wall and corners were scrubbed clean, I hung costumes to air. If I saw any damage, I alerted the tiring-man in charge of costumes, and he would get it mended. If it was valuable or delicate, I placed it in a basket for young Mistress Dippity. She was trusted with the finest needlework. I liked it when she came, because she always brought me something tasty to eat, and a bone for Hoppy.

I was exhausted by the end of the day but happy to be soaking up the life of the playhouse and the players.

Nothing they gave me to do put me off wanting to be part of that life. But still I yearned to act.

One evening, Master Shakespeare came

across while I was sitting on the ground, teaching Hoppy to roll over.

I looked up and said, 'I should never have run away. It was all for nothing.'

'Why so?'

'I missed my chance to be on stage,' I said. 'I truly thought it would be the beginning of me learning to be a player. All I wanted to do was walk on and act – I didn't expect to have words to say. Not yet. And now it's over, all because everyone is angry with me.'

Expecting him to walk away, I looked down and, without thinking, I flipped my hand, telling Hoppy to do a somersault. He obediently jumped over backwards. I signalled to him to do it again.

Some passing players laughed at Hoppy. 'That was good, Billy,' said one.

Then Master Shakespeare's voice said, 'What a clever dog. Can he do anything else?'

'He can die for the king,' I said, and gave the signal, two quick pats of my hand on my leg. Hoppy flopped down and lay on his side as if dead.

'Call him,' I said. 'He will not move until he hears my signal.'

One of the players tried. Hoppy stayed still.

'I know what will shift him,' said another, reaching into his leather bag. He pulled out a lamb cutlet and waved it over Hoppy's nose.

Nothing.

They tried all sorts of teases, but Hoppy didn't move. Finally, I clicked with my tongue and Hoppy leapt into life.

'Remarkable, isn't he, Will?' said a player.

Master Shakespeare looked thoughtful. 'He certainly is. Get some rest, Billy-Odd-Job,' he said. 'Master Burbage and I want you at rehearsals tomorrow.'

My legs went weak. 'Do you mean—?'

He smiled. 'You've been punished enough. Tomorrow morning you will be in the rehearsal for the marketplace scene in *Romeo and Juliet*.' He bent to stroke Hoppy. 'Your dog can be there, too. It would be natural for a boy to take his dog to market. This little beast is well behaved enough.'

A wave of happiness washed over me. I grabbed Hoppy and hugged him and this time my tears were real.

CHAPTER TWELVE

I spent a wakeful night. Not because of scuttling rats – because of joy. My dream was about to come true.

I could not eat the breakfast old John Merry brought me. I was desperate for rehearsals to begin.

When everyone had arrived, Master Burbage said, 'Those who do not have a speaking part must be on stage as bystanders.'

Then he told me, 'You must pretend to buy fruit from that stall.'

I looked where he pointed. 'What stall?'

'For rehearsal, you must imagine it. We shall see how well you act, boy.' He turned away. 'I want Sampson, Gregory and Abraham to speak their lines. Benvolio, once they start fighting, be ready to break in.' He looked around. 'We have acted this play many times. Today, pretend it's the first time – make it come alive!'

It was my first time, and even though it was only a rehearsal, my hands shook. Master Shakespeare stood in the shadows, watching. William Shakespeare, watching me!

One of the players whispered, 'I'm the fruit seller, Billy. Talk to me without making a sound. Just move your lips.'

I nodded. When Master Burbage said, 'Begin!' I picked up a pretend apple, looked at it and put it back. I was aware of the players behind me speaking their parts, but I tried to imagine myself to be someone just shopping in the market. I examined more fruit, and picked up a pear. Without making a sound, I asked the fruit seller how much it was. I don't know what he said back, but I shook my head as if it was too expensive.

Suddenly there was a commotion behind me. Swords clashed. How should I act? If this were real, I would turn and look. I did so, then darted backwards as if I was afraid I might be hurt.

Master Burbage strode to the middle of the stage. 'Stop!' he cried. 'You call this a fight? You are like children hitting each other with rattles. Everyone else leave the stage. We must work on this fight if we are to convince tomorrow's audience that you are even the slightest bit annoyed at each other.'

My first rehearsal had lasted a matter of minutes.

But then, Master Burbage leaned over and said, 'You did well, Billy.' He looked over my shoulder. 'Did he not, Will?'

I spun round. Master Shakespeare smiled. 'He did indeed. You have the instincts of a true player.'

I felt warm inside. Those words, from the greatest playwright in the land, meant so much.

I did my morning tasks. Not even being sneered at by Nick Ratter made them hard. In fact, they had never seemed so light and easy.

After our meal break, the players went to dress for the afternoon performance, then people began arriving, clutching pennies for the box man. The groundlings, standing in the yard, had the best view in my opinion.

They loved to cheer and jeer and bandy words with the players.

As I showed richer people to their seats, the food sellers came in to sell their wares. Soon the aromas of hot pies and roast chestnuts mixed with the fresh tang of oranges. I closed my eyes, breathed it all in, the smells, the chatter and laughter from the crowd and thought, for the hundredth time, 'I love everything about the playhouse. This is where I want to spend my life.' I could not bear the thought of becoming a secretary like my father, doing the same dreary tasks day after day.

When the play began, I took a moment to nip outside to let Hoppy cock his leg. As I walked back in, a hand touched my shoulder.

I turned.

'Mother!'

CHAPTER THIRTEEN

I closed my eyes waiting for the blow, but it never came. When I opened them, I saw no anger in my mother's face.

I took her hand. 'I missed you. But I had to come. I had to have my chance, and tomorrow I will.'

She spoke for the first time. 'I have opened up the house and lit the fires. Come home now, Billy. Wash and put on clean clothes. You smell like a street child.'

'But I am working, Mother.' I took a deep breath. 'Tomorrow I am to play a bystander, on stage.'

'Wonderful.' She did not sound thrilled. This was hardly surprising as she never liked me being at the playhouse. I wondered, just for a moment, hadn't Father ever talked to her about following your heart?

'You will work better after good hot food,' she said. 'Come. Susan longs to see you.'

I fancied I could smell beef stew on her clothing. Suddenly, I yearned for comfort.

'I'm glad Susan is well,' I said. 'I have kept her in my prayers.'

I hadn't, which made me feel doubly bad.

I found old John Merry and explained where I was going.

'I'm right glad your mother is back,' he said. 'I hope she is not too angry with you.'

'She is not angry at all,' I said happily.

Life was good. I was going to have my home again, and I would play my first part in public the very next day.

I called Hoppy and we all three set off for home. The weather was bright and clear. I decided I would pray for good weather on the morrow. If it was too wet, there would be no performance.

As we walked, I noticed grass and weeds growing among the cobbles. 'What has happened to the road?' I asked.

'So many people left London because of the plague that the roads have not been well used,' replied my mother. 'Even though the plague is officially over, it does not mean that it's not still here.'

I noticed that she carried a pomander of herbs and spices, which she held to her nose whenever the path grew crowded. She was still afraid of catching plague.

I saw more signs of the disease. Houses with windows boarded up against thieves, and doors with red crosses painted on them.

We turned into Little Thames Lane, and I saw smoke rising from our chimney. How good it felt to see our own house! Hoppy's new home!

Mother opened the door. I stood inside and sniffed familiar smells: fire smoke, food cooking, lavender, and herbs mixed in with floor rushes, crushed beneath my feet. Our rooms were bigger and airier than Aunt Meg's, and our furniture shone, whereas hers was roughened wood. Through a room at the back I glimpsed our garden, where everything had grown while we had been away. Roses had gone wild, rambling over dried-looking bean plants.

I heard a key turn and the clunk of a lock.

I spun round. Mother had locked the door.

She put the key in the pocket she wore inside her kirtle and said in a cold, hard voice. 'How … *dare* … you!'

'Wha— what?'

'How DARE you run away and cause me such agony? I thought my heart would *break*. You disappeared without a word. How … DARE you!'

She thumped the table with clenched fists.

I backed away.

'Did you give one thought to what your aunt and uncle and I would think? We didn't know if you had been attacked and left to freeze in a ditch. We didn't know if you were murdered. How could you leave like that?'

'But – but I left a letter,' I protested. 'Did you not see it?'

'What letter? I saw no letter.'

'It was in pictures,' I said. 'It explained where I was going, and it ended with the pictures that said, "I love you"... and I do,' I added, hoping to calm her. 'I left it on the table.'

'Then whoever picked it up would have assumed it was one of the drawings you always left around the place. I only discovered where you were when we received Master Shakespeare's letter.' She threw a log on the fire. 'Go and see Susan, then go to your bedroom. There is water there. Wash yourself and put on fresh clothes.'

'Yes, Mother.'

'Then come down and help with the

cleaning. Spiders and mice have moved in while we've been away, and I want neither in this house.'

'Yes, Mother.'

My sister was fast asleep with a strange curly-haired girl beside her.

'Who are you?' I asked.

'Nelly,' she said. 'Your mother's new maid. You're Billy.'

I stared at her. 'I know.'

'I got to keep an eye on you,' she said, making both pale eyes round and staring.

I decided she was daft, and turned to Susan. She looked much better than when I saw her last. I stroked her cheek. Her little hand touched mine.

'Billy,' she said, and I thought she smiled a little.

When I was clean, I went downstairs. The rest of the day passed in a flurry of brooms and wet cloths and anger in the air.

Finally we stopped for a bowl of stew and fresh bread. It was delicious. When I was full, I tried to start a conversation.

'How was your journey home, Mother?'

She had calmed, but I could see she was still angry.

'I will talk to you in the morning,' she said. 'Go to bed.'

As I turned towards the stairs I found Nelly sitting on the third step, staring at me.

'What are you doing?' I asked.

'Keeping an eye on you,' she replied, and followed me to the door of my room.

'I hope you can see through wood,' I said, slamming the door in her face.

Her footsteps faded, then I heard my mother's footsteps coming closer.

A key turned.

I was locked in!

'Mother!' I called. 'Why have you locked me in?'

'You ran away,' she said. 'You must be punished.'

'But you'll let me out in the morning?' I asked.

There was no reply.

'Mother!' I said frantically. 'The play is tomorrow!'

She'd gone. I sat on the bed with my head in my hands.

The next thing I heard was scuffling at the door, then Nelly's spiteful voice whispered, 'No plays for you.'

CHAPTER FOURTEEN

I slept in fits and starts. It was so unfair. I was only trying to do what my father and Will Shakespeare did – to follow my heart. But always something stopped me.

I understood, I truly did, why Mother didn't want me to mix with players. She thought they were bad people. Well, some of them do drink too much, and sometimes they are unkind to their lady friends, but they all love poetry and plays. There would *be* no plays without people like Will Shakespeare and Richard Burbage. They are from good, hard-working families and Master Shakespeare could not write such beautiful words if he was a bad man.

They cannot be so terrible if a queen and a king have had them play in their palaces.

I couldn't let my chance slip by again, even if it meant severe punishment afterwards. I would follow my heart, and my heart was leading me to the Globe.

I decided to escape by jumping from my window. The bushes below had grown wild and straggly while we were away. They would cushion my fall. I opened the window to see the drop.

The bushes were there, but so was an enormous brown and black dog, tethered to a post. I knew that dog. Its name was Gruff, and it belonged to the silversmith around the corner. He used it to keep thieves away.

Mother must have guessed what I might try to do, and borrowed the dog to stop me. It looked up.

'Grrrr.'

How lucky, I thought, that I am good with dogs.

'Gruff!' I called. 'Gruffy!'

I reckoned if the dog jumped up, I could reach down and pat his head.

I leaned out as far as I dared. He jumped up and I stretched my hand out.

'Grrrrarrghh!'

He nearly took my hand off! No one could make friends with that great brute.

I sank back on my bed, just as the key turned. The door opened slightly. A plate of bread and cold beef was pushed through the gap, together with a cup of small beer.

A pale eye peered at me.

'Hee hee, I'm keeping an eye on you,' said Nelly.

She backed out and locked the door.

There was a dead spider on the beef, with strings of fly-specked web attached. Nelly must have put it there, the spiteful, lump-headed baggage.

I took the meat to the window. Why hadn't I realized, you have to get a fierce dog to like you before you can be friends? What better way than to feed it?

'Here, Gruffy!' I called.

The dog turned its glittering black eyes on me as I held out the beef. He sniffed and jumped up.

I dropped the meat into his open, slobbery mouth.

With one gulp, it was gone.

I tried to pat his head again. 'Here, Gruff!'

'Grrrrarrghh!'

Ungrateful animal. I'd lost my breakfast for nothing. Now what?

It was bad enough being forbidden to act in the play but, I realized, what was just as awful was that Masters Shakespeare and Burbage might think I didn't care enough to turn up and play my part.

A gentle voice floated through my open window. 'Hello, Gruff. Why are you here?'

I knew that voice. I flew to the window.

It was Dippity, who does the important needlework for the Globe. She was stroking Gruff!

'Mistress Dippity,' I called.

She looked up, smiling. The dog growled, but she rubbed his ears and said, 'Silly Gruff.'

He quietened.

'Good day, Billy-Odd-Job,' she said. 'I hear you are to play a part today, and Hoppy, too.

I am glad for you.'

'Mistress Dippity,' I said, 'Are you going to the Globe?'

Nodding, she lifted the cloth covering her basket. Inside was a bundle of lace.

'Would you give a message to Master Shakespeare or Master Burbage?' I asked.

She looked troubled. 'I do not remember things easily, Billy-Odd-Job.'

'Can you carry a letter?' I asked.

'Oh yes,' she said.

I took some charcoal and paper and wrote.

Dear Mstr Shakespeare & Mstr Burbage, my mother has locked me in for running away and will not let me out to play my part. I am sorry. It has broken my heart. Please don't think badly of me. From Billy.

'Here,' I said, throwing it down and praying Gruff wouldn't eat it. 'You won't lose it, will you?' I was slightly worried.

I know she finds many simple tasks difficult.

'I won't,' she said. 'See? It is in my hand.'

'Thank you, Mistress Dippity.'

When she had gone, I lay down on my bed. At least the players would know the truth.

I felt tearful again. Then I must have slept.

CHAPTER FIFTEEN

Gruff's furious barking woke me. I heard footsteps outside, and a man's voice yelling firmly, 'Down!'

I seemed to recognize the voice, but I dozed off again.

The next thing I knew was the key turning in the lock, and my mother saying, 'Billy, come downstairs. Now.'

I sat up. She looked hot and flustered.

'What is it?'

'Come *now*!'

I followed her downstairs.

Who should be sitting beside the fire, stroking Hoppy, but William Shakespeare!

'Good evening, sir,' I said, for I could tell by the light that it was getting late.

While Mother lit some candles, I whispered

to Master Shakespeare, 'Did Dippity—'

He put a finger to his lips and nodded, then said aloud, 'When you did not turn up today, I wondered if you were ill, Billy. I am glad you are not.'

'No, I—'

'I have persuaded your mother to forgive you for running away to join the company. She knows that I was minded to do the same thing once.'

I looked from one to the other. I swear my mother blushed.

'Will and I knew each other when we were young,' she said softly. 'He married another, then disappeared for a while, and I – I married his closest friend.'

My eyes nearly popped from my head. Was my mother once in love with William Shakespeare?

As he accepted a cup of wine from her, Master Shakespeare said, 'I remember what it was like to want to go on the stage so badly that I would do anything to achieve it – even leave home.'

Mother cleared her throat. 'Will tells me that you, Billy, are a promising young actor, and the keenest he has known for years. But I cannot have you hanging around the Globe waiting for parts between sweeping and fetching and carrying for people.'

To my dismay, Master Shakespeare said, 'I agree.'

'Oh,' said I, feeling sick and hopeless.

'So,' he continued, 'with your mother's blessing, you will be apprenticed to one of the finest players in the company. You will learn to—'

He talked on, but I barely heard a word, I was so full of joy. I hugged my mother. 'Oh, thank you!' I hugged my dog. I only just stopped myself from hugging Master Shakespeare!

I saw Nelly's eyes as big as frying eggs, peering through the stairway, but I cared not a jot for her. I was to be a player!

But what was Master Shakespeare saying?

'...there is one condition. If you do not agree to it, the King's Men cannot accept you.'

My stomach turned over. 'What is the condition, sir?'

'Hoppy must join the company, too. We have not seen so comical and clever an animal since Will Kempe and his dog left, years ago. There is a part for Hoppy as Launce's dog, Crab, in *Two Gentlemen of Verona*. Can you teach your signals to the man who plays Launce?'

I laughed. 'I can indeed, sir!'

I had heard of Will Kempe and his dog. When Master Kempe left the Chamberlain's Men, he danced all the way to Norwich – more than a hundred miles – and called his dance the 'Nine Days' Wonder!' He didn't dance it all in one go, of course, but rested between each of the dance days.

While Will Shakespeare and Mother talked awhile of things past, I stared into the fire, thinking of the wonderful future before me.

Eventually, Master Shakespeare stood. He looked down at me. 'Well, Billy-Odd-Job, we must call you by your proper name now. William Watkins, apprentice player!'

That sounded so good! But it wasn't *exactly* what I wanted.

'If you please, sir,' I said. 'I would like to be known as Will. Will Watkins.'

He laughed and clapped me on the back. 'It is a fine name – Will!'

★

Mother was the guest of William Shakespeare at my first performance. She had an honoured seat in the lords' room, and old John Merry was to sit beside her, so that no one should bother her.

She told me there would be a surprise for me after the performance, but I was too excited to take much notice. I was to be in the first scene of Act Three as well as in Act One, and I would be on stage again at the end when the audience would cheer us.

And so it happened. The only thing that concerned me was that when I glanced up at my mother, old John Merry was not beside her – I could not see his white beard gleaming in the shadows. I could barely make out my mother's features at all, but she seemed composed.

When the play was over and it had been as wonderful as I had dreamt, Master Shakespeare came to me in the tiring house.

'I wish you a long and successful career,

Will Watkins,' he said. 'And by the way, I noticed that the letter you sent with Mistress Dippity was written with charcoal. I would like you to have this, to bring you luck.'

He took from his little table his ink jar and a quill.

I caught my breath. 'Thank you, sir. Is this your own quill?'

He nodded. 'It is my second best. It writes well. And now, your mother is outside, waiting to congratulate you. She has a surprise for you.'

I had thought that the ink and quill were my surprise. I went outside and ran down the steps to hug Mother. But she was not alone. There was a man with her, a sun-browned man with long curling dark hair and an untidy beard.

I could not believe my eyes. 'Father!' I cried. 'Oh, Father!'

He held out his arms.

'When did you get home?' I asked, my voice shaking.

'This morning,' he replied, hugging me close.

I clung to him, smelling the sea on him. Then my tears began to fall. 'Father, I did it,' I sobbed. 'I followed my heart!'

I have never been so happy.

EPILOGUE

Will Watkins joined the right acting company! The Globe became hugely successful, with packed audiences including visitors from the country and foreign travellers. For a great afternoon's entertainment you only needed a penny for the doorman's box. (Ever wondered why today's theatres have 'box' offices?)

Nine years later, disaster struck when the company's cannon was fired during a performance, setting light to the thatched roof. But the Globe was rebuilt – with a tiled roof – and reopened a year later.

Then, in 1642, Parliament closed the playhouses. The Globe was pulled down to make way for new housing. However, that wasn't the end. Visit London today and you, too, can experience Shakespeare in the reconstructed Globe Theatre.